Dear Parents,

Congratulations! Your child has embarked on an exciting journey – they're learning to read! As a parent, you can be there to support and cheer them along as they take their first steps.

At school, children are taught how to decode words and arrange these building blocks of language into sentences and wonderful stories.

At home, parents play a vital part in reinforcing these new-found skills. You can help your child practise their reading by providing well-written, engaging stories, which you can enjoy together.

This series – **Ready, Steady, Read!** – offers exactly that, and more. These stories support inexperienced readers by:

- gradually introducing new vocabulary
- using repetition to consolidate learning
- gradually increasing sentence length and word count
- providing texts that boost a young reader's confidence.

As each book is completed, engaging activities encourage young readers to look back at the story, while a Picture Dictionary reinforces new vocabulary. Enjoyment is the key – and reading together can be great fun for both parent and child!

Prue Goodwin
Lecturer in Literacy and Children's Books

The **Ready, Steady, Read!** series has 4 levels.
The facing page shows what you can expect to find
in the books at each level.

As your child's confidence grows, they can progress
to books from the higher levels. These will keep them
engaged and encourage new reading skills.

The levels are only meant as guides; together, you and
your child can pick the book that will be just right.

Here are some handy tips for helping children who are
ready for reading!

Give them choice – Letting children pick a book
(from the level that's right for them) makes them
feel involved.

Talk about it – Discussing the story and the
pictures helps children engage with the book.

Read it again – Repetition of favourite stories
reinforces learning.

Cheer them on! – Praise and encouragement
builds a child's confidence and the belief in their
growing ability.

LEVEL 1 For first readers

* short, straightforward sentences
* basic, fun vocabulary
* simple, easy-to-follow stories of up to 100 words
* large print and easy-to-read design

LEVEL 2 For developing readers

* longer sentences
* simple vocabulary, introducing new words
* longer stories of up to 200 words
* bold design, to capture readers' interest

LEVEL 3 For more confident readers

* longer sentences with varied structure
* wider vocabulary
* high-interest stories of up to 300 words
* smaller print for experienced readers

LEVEL 4 For able readers

* longer sentences with complex structure
* rich, exciting vocabulary
* complex stories of up to 400 words
* emphasis on text more than illustrations

Make Reading Fun!

Once you have read the story, you will find some amazing activities at the back of the book! There are Excellent Exercises for you to complete, plus a super Picture Dictionary.

But first it is time for the story . . .

Ready?
Steady?
Let's read!

Julia Rawlinson   Tim Warnes

Rosie's Special Surprise

LITTLE TIGER PRESS
London

Nosy Rosie liked
to know *everything*.

So when Daddy Rabbit
said he had a big surprise . . .

. . . Rosie went to
look for it.

Rosie found some acorns.

"That is not your surprise,"
said Squirrel.

Rosie kept looking . . .

. . . until she found
a tunnel.

"That is not your surprise," said the moles.

Rosie looked . . .

and looked.

She found
a nest.

"That is not
your surprise,"
said the birds.

Rosie hopped up the hill . . .

. . . and fell back down again.

"*Where* is my surprise?"
said Rosie sadly.

"Come with me,"
said Daddy.

"It's a big, blue balloon!
Oooh – thank you!" said
Rosie. "Now I can see . . ."

"... EVERYTHING!"

Excellent Exercises

Have you read the story? Well done! Now it is time for more fun!

Here are some questions about the story. Ask an adult to listen to your answers, and help if you get stuck.

Special Surprise

In this story, Daddy Rabbit has a surprise for Rosie. Have *you* ever had a special surprise?

Brilliant Balloon

Can you name all the things that Rosie can see in this picture? What kind of things would *you* like to see from a hot air balloon?

Amazing Adventure

Now describe what Rosie is doing in this picture.

Hidden Treasures

Can you remember what Rosie finds first? What do *you* like to look for when you go on a walk?

Picture Dictionary

Can you read all of these words from the story?

acorns

balloon

birds

blue

fell

hill

moles

nest

squirrel

tunnel

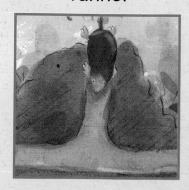

Can you think of any other words that describe these
pictures – for example, what colours can you see? Why
not try to spell some of these words? Ask an adult to help!

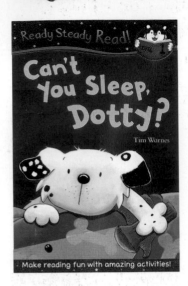

Can't You Sleep, Dotty?

Dotty has tried everything. But she just cannot sleep. Soon all her friends are trying to help her. But will anything work . . . ?

Fred

Fred has a new little door. It's called a cat flap. But Fred knows that Horrible Henry is waiting outside, ready to pounce . . . !

My Turn!

When Oscar and Tilly go to the playground, they are not keen to wait their turn. Will the two friends find a way to play together?

What Bear Likes Best!

Bear really likes to have fun. But all of his friends are busy and he keeps getting in the way! Will it ever be time to play?

For Ben and Tom, with love — J R
For Ethan, who surprised everyone by being so early — T W

LITTLE TIGER PRESS, 1 The Coda Centre, 189 Munster Road, London SW6 6AW
First published in Great Britain 2005
This edition published 2013
Text copyright © Julia Rawlinson 2005, 2013
Illustrations copyright © Tim Warnes 2005, 2013
Printed in China
978-1-84895-666-7
LTP/1800/0587/0413
2 4 6 8 10 9 7 5 3 1

LEVEL 1 - For first readers

Can't You Sleep, Dotty?

Fred

My Turn!

Rosie's Special Surprise

What Bear Likes Best!

LEVEL 2 - For developing readers

Hopping Mad!

Newton

Ouch!

Where There's a Bear, There's Trouble!

The Wish Cat

LEVEL 3 - For more confident readers

Lazy Ozzie

Little Mouse and the Big Red Apple

Nobody Laughs at a Lion!

Ridiculous!

Who's Been Eating My Porridge?

LEVEL 4 - For able readers

The Biggest Baddest Wolf

Meggie Moon

Mouse, Mole and the Falling Star

The Nutty Nut Chase

Robot Dog